WHAT LIVING AND DYING IS LIKE

TWO SHORT STORIES

IAIN RYAN

LAMBHOUSE

Praise for IAIN RYAN

"An exciting new voice in Australian crime fiction" – Adrian McKinty, author of *The Chain*

"One of Australia's most interesting next-gen crime writers." — Sue Turnbull, *The Sydney Morning Herald*

"Iain Ryan ducks your defences and gets in close to deliver literary habit punches to the kidneys that'll leave you bleeding and eager for more punishment." — Jedidiah Ayres, author of *Peckerwood* and *Fierce Bitches*

"Iain Ryan has learned the lessons of the modern maestros James Ellroy, Ken Bruen, and James Sallis, but his poetry and cadence is completely Australian." — Peter Doyle, author of *The Big Whatever* and *Crooks Like Us*

For Clare

RUSTY

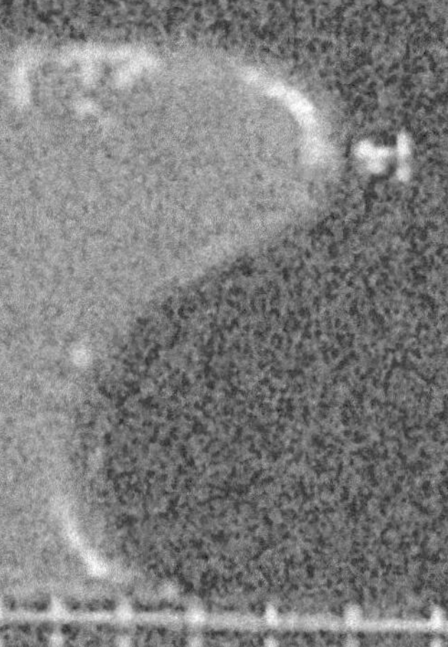

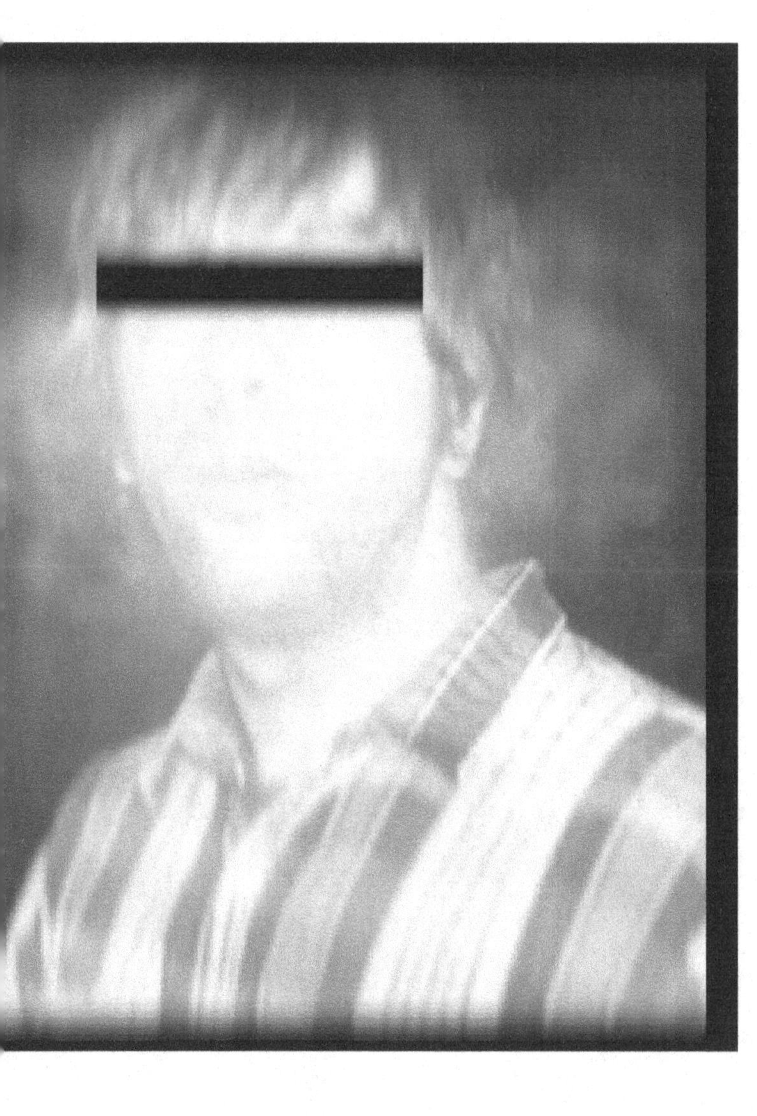

What is not brought to consciousness
comes to us as fate.

— Carl Jung

Chapter One

The machine buzzed and Rusty watched the coffee trickle out. He started to wonder. Winter had passed like a daydream. December, January, February, all blank. *How does a person forget December? What did I do the week of Christmas? The week after Christmas?* He assumed he slept, ate, and commuted. He assumed he sat here at his desk in the tech office and that the lecturers called down and the students signed the logbook. It all must have happened, but where was he throughout all this? *Did it snow? Did the wind blow?*

Rusty walked to his computer and stared at the screen. *eBay could fix this. eBay kept a record.* Rusty looked at the entries and a picture of his lost months started to develop: a Yamaha SPX-900 sampler arrived in December. It came with a Sanyo cassette Walkman and a repress of *Loveless*. January brought the Criterion edition of *Silence of the Lambs* and a 308 chip for a cheap *Rat* pedal. Rusty stared at the rest of the list and tried to picture where it all was now, and where it all came from. He opened his most recent purchases. There was a guitar. It was hazard-light orange. He studied the hardware and joinery and had a weird feeling about it. The guitar wasn't right, but it was too bright to ignore.

Chapter Two

On Thursday, the orange guitar arrived and was given its own chair in the living room. Everyone in the house sat there and looked at it. Rusty sparked up a joint and passed it to his room-mate Charger, who shook his head and said, "I'm cooked." Charger moved the joint on to his girl-friend, a Minnesotan woman, the name of whom Rusty had forgotten. She was new.

"Why d'you get an orange one?" she said. She shuffled forward on the couch. "Nothing goes with orange."

"I don't know," said Rusty.

"It's just too fucking orange," said Charger.

"Yeah," said the woman. "Do you even play guitar?"

Charger ran his hands down his thighs, suddenly tense. "I told you about Rusty's old band."

"That's right," said the woman. "I forgot."

Rusty took another hit. "I'm putting something together. But with that thing, I just wanted it, so I bought it." He could feel his voice drawing out as he spoke.

Charger picked up the TV remote and changed the channel, as if this might also change the conversation, but nothing was on. *Family Ties*, basketball highlights, home shopping. Still flicking, he mentioned that the rent was due, and that Sarah called, and then he told a story about an upstairs neighbour, a weird little guy who fancied himself a DJ. This was the news of the day.

"Sounds like a busy one," said Rusty.

Charger didn't really have a job. He freelanced as a personal trainer but never seemed to have regulars. Instead, he had a silver credit card that appeared whenever financial trouble arose. His parents did something in mining.

"I'm getting tired," said Rusty.

They all did shots.

The woman rolled another joint. As she licked the paper, she looked again at the guitar. "You know, my little sister buys weird shit like that online. She buys stuff about... just music stuff, I guess. You should hang out with her. You two might get along. She's kinda fucking weird too."

"Katrina, what do you mean by that?" said Charger.

Katrina. That was it.

Rusty laughed. "It's okay."

Katrina didn't seem to notice. "It's *so* fucking weird man. My sister is like, competitive and shit with it. She fucking *hates* this other girl who snaps up stuff she wants on eBay. This other girl is like that fucking baby with the mono brow in the Simpsons, you know? Like her nemesis."

Rusty said, "What's she buying?"

"Oh man, you know that band Couleurs? Their stuff."

"How old is she?" said Charger.

'She's...' Katrina closed her eyes. 'She's like, nineteen."

"Why is she buying boy band shit if she's nineteen?"

Katrina stood up, excited. "Because that bitch sells it on to other people on the internet."

Charger looked like he was about to green out. He did not like this story. "No," he said. "I don't know what that is." Charger wasn't good at the internet or business.

Rusty didn't like the story either. He let himself slide down into the lounge a little. Something felt off. Katrina was about to say something really fucked up.

"And do you know what my sister told me? She's got this one customer, this super fucking messed up lady who buys stuff because she thinks she can see people's secrets, just by touching their used things from eBay. She reckons she knows everything about this Couleurs band because she's touched some drumstick or some sweaty towel of theirs, you know? How weird is that? How weird is it?"

Charger put his face in his hands. He strived to live completely within the physical world and hated the supernatural. "She can't ever come over here," he said.

Katrina laughed. "Who?"

"That woman."

They all saw the gears grinding in Charger's mind. He was suddenly in a place where nothing was private.

"It's okay, man," said Rusty, but it got him thinking.

Chapter Three

Katrina lived with her sister in a townhouse just off campus. They were both enrolled at UNLV, both in business.

"Did you study?" Katrina said, in the car, on the way over.

"Yeah," said Rusty. "But you know."

"It's rough."

"You sure your sister will be okay with me dropping round like this?"

"Let me see... My guess is she'll be sitting with her computer in her pyjamas. Trust me, she needs to have a conversation with a real person. She probably hasn't spoken to anyone since term ended."

"What's her name again?"

"Elsa."

As reported, Elsa sat at the kitchen table in front of a battered black laptop.

"Hey dickhead, we've got company," said Katrina as they stepped inside.

Elsa ignored it.

"This is Rusty. He's Charger's room-mate."

"What's a Charger?" Elsa said.

"This guy I've been seeing. Jesus El, why do you have to be such a retard? Go put some fucking pants on?"

Elsa turned and looked over. "Rusty, do you mind if I wear what I want in my own house? Is that going to be a big thing for you?"

"Maybe I should come back?" said Rusty.

In a way that seemed routine, Katrina went to the table and closed her sister's laptop. "Rusty has just come over here so you can tell him about how you sell shit on the internet. So go and put some pants on, then come back out and be a normal human being, or I will tell Dad you did meth."

"That's—"

"Uh-uh." Katrina knocked a finger against the table. "That's how it is. Now, go."

Elsa went.

Katrina clapped her hands together. "Don't worry about her. She's like that with everyone." In a low whisper she added, "I think she's shy."

This did not prove to be correct. Once dressed, Elsa puffed on a cigarette and explained to Rusty how she bought and sold music memorabilia online. She talked about her research and description copy, and how she saw Couleurs coming up long before the rest of the eBay hawks. It all started as a term paper. "I don't really like the band," she said. "I think that helps. All I care about is the money. Which is great because all these girls care about is the band. It's a perfect market."

"Do you buy anything for yourself?"

"Not really. I don't really like eBay either."

When they started comparing bidding software, Katrina grew bored. She moved to the couch and checked her phone, then announced she was leaving. As soon as she left, Elsa reopened the laptop and began typing. The conversation was over, apparently. Unsure of what to do with himself, Rusty paced around. He stared out at the townhouse's courtyard. It needed work. Shrubs tumbled out of beds, unkept grass sprouting up. Three brittle dead plants sat in pots by the sliding door of the balcony.

"I think my sister was hoping we'd hook up," Elsa said.

"Really?"

"I guess. She does this from time to time."

"Do you have a boyfriend?"

"What? No," Elsa said. "Do you?"

"No," said Rusty. "I'm not—"

"You know what I meant."

"Yeah," he said, and the rest of weekend seemed to expand out from there, from that tiny word travelling across the room.

Chapter Four

The orange guitar was still in the living room chair when Rusty arrived home. Charger left the television on. Rusty stood and watched the screen's reflection in the bright enamel finish.

The next morning, Rusty scanned his eBay profile. There was now no trace of the orange guitar's seller in his account details. It was gone. Rusty tapped out a letter to the site and asked for an explanation. As he wrote, his heart beat a little faster from his breakfast coffee, and from the weekend, and from some things he remembered from Elsa's bedroom. He wrote, *Why has this seller disappeared?*

The guitar stayed in its chair in the living room for a week until Charger brought friends back and they needed space to party. Someone, Katrina probably, tucked the guitar under the covers of Rusty's bed, laying the headstock on the pillow as if it were sleeping. That night, faced with a night on the couch, Rusty was forced to pick up the guitar for the first time. It felt okay in his hands. It was out of tune, but he strummed a few chords anyhow. It sounded nice. He had a small practise amp in his room and plugged it in.

Chapter Five

For a month, Rusty worked in the tech office, smoked weed, and wrote songs. He found an open tuning the guitar seemed to like and a vocabulary of chords tumbled out. He sang for the first time in years and while singing was never his strong suit, his voice sat well with the orange guitar. It all worked together, as if the guitar were a flashlight dragging the rest behind.

Rusty wrote and sang about the tiny world around him. He sang about his lime green office at work, about the books he bought online and the characters in them. He sang about the Vegas strip and the suburbs, and about his parents as young people and their car and the house and his sister. His family had come across the desert through the heat. He also remembered the wooden chairs in junior high, the skate park, the kids he met, all long gone. In his memories, Fiona and her twin sister Carmen swam naked in the neighbour's pool. He recalled this and the way Brian lit his cigarettes and the way sitting in Allan's car felt. He even visited Elsa through these new songs, writing lines of verses and choruses for a girl he barely knew, whom he hadn't called or spoken to since their first meeting. All of this came out of the orange guitar.

Late one night after a session, Rusty sat outside and smoked and thought about it. *It was funny how things changed without signal.* The days felt longer now. He felt better about them. Still downcast about where he was and how it all started, but better, clearer maybe. The orange guitar was just lumber and wire, but it was helping where nothing else had for a while.

Why?

Rusty returned to his room and spoke to the guitar, "Where did you come from?"

It took a good long moment to think through the rest of it, but an idea appeared. And while the answer didn't please him any, he felt completely indebted to this idea from the first glimmer. It was a direction of sorts.

Chapter Six

"Oh right. You're back," said Elsa, opening the door.

"I've been busy."

"So I hear. Hiding in your room. Come in, I guess."

Elsa sat at the table and tapped the space bar. She was dressed the same as last time, in a pyjama top and black cotton underwear.

"I want to ask you about a story your sister told me."

Elsa's eyes remained on the screen.

"Your sister said something about one of your customers, a girl who buys a lot of the same stuff. She said..."

"I'm listening."

"She said this girl can see things from touching stuff, the stuff she buys online, like a clairvoyant."

"Uh-huh. That's what she told me once. She's a fucking idiot. But an idiot with lots of money. The worst kind of idiot, really. Or the best. I don't know." Elsa continued typing. "I could give you her email address. But why?"

"I have something I need checked out."

"Then you're an idiot too. I know she lives in Dallas. Dallas is where the packages go."

Rusty took out his phone. "Can I have the address?"

Elsa looked at him. She rolled a hand around on her wrist, stretching the muscles. "I want a bag of weed," she said.

"Done."

"Okay. It's three couleurs — the band name — blue, all one word, at gmail dot com."

"Thanks."

"What are you going to do?" she said.

"I'm going to go see her, I guess. It's about this guitar I have."

Elsa nodded. "Katrina told me you were obsessed with that thing." She turned back to the laptop. "Do you think you might come back sometime?"

He stood up. "Yeah, I mean, I've been…"

"Do you have to go now?"

He didn't, but he said yes.

Chapter Seven

Charger was not impressed when he heard about the trip to Dallas to see the clairvoyant. "Dude, she could be a fucking serial killer. She could have a gimp in the basement. She might need another one. You might never come back, bro." He was still in his gym clothes, but had a small bong in his hand. Charger always needed a cone in moments of duress. He loved to make things worse.

"It's fine," said Rusty. "I looked her up on Facebook. She's just some kid."

"That's what people do. That's how they find their victims. I read about this girl pretending to be this young hot babe on the internet and it turns out she was this fucked up mom. Not cool."

Rusty returned to his packing. "I'm pretty sure that was a movie we watched."

"She's going to want to touch more than your guitar, that's my prediction. You should take some, like, mace or something."

"I'm not flying all the way to Dallas to mace a clairvoyant. I've never been to Dallas."

"I don't like it," Charger said. "And Dallas fucking sucks."

"I'll be fine."

"Yeah, whatever," he said, taking another short toke on the bong. "I think I might go to the shop. I'm gonna get beer, no, a frozen pizza. No, beer."

Rusty said, "I need a lift to the airport."

Charger pretended to punch Rusty's bedroom door, "Uh, uh, uh." When he was finished, he shook his head and said, "I guess I can do both."

Chapter Eight

The eBay clairvoyant's name was Ava Wells. Rusty hired a car at DFW and drove to where Ava lived, about halfway between the terminal and the city. She refused to meet him anywhere else. Her house was a nondescript brick place. It sat in the back corner of a new, silent estate, under a grey cloudless sky.

Rusty knocked on the door.

The woman who opened up wore denim cut-off shorts and a sleeveless flannelette shirt. She was impossibly thin, almost frail-looking, and was made more so by long, ghostly white hair.

"Yes?"

"I'm Rusty, from the internet."

"Did you bring cash?"

"Yeah."

Ava did not move from the door.

"I'll get it," he said, crouching down to open his pack.

Ava took the money and counted it off. "Good one. Leave your shoes on. We'll go out back."

The house was as empty as a display home and smelled like dust and mildew.

"What do you do?" Rusty said. "For work."

"I write."

"In here?"

"In there." She pointed to a closed door as they passed by.

They cut through a long empty living room and out into the yard. Ava had a small paved area with plastic outdoor chairs and a table. "Pop it up here." She took a pair of sunglasses from her pocket and lit a smoke. "Orange, huh?"

"So how does this work? Do you need some time with it?"

"No, not normally. But I find it helps if I have a poke around and let it sit a while. I'll message you with whatever comes to me. You can take the guitar today though, I don't need it. Shit, I really don't need *this* thing lying around."

Then Ava put her hands on the guitar, one flat on the body, the other resting on the neck, cigarette still between her fingers. She closed her eyes and hummed to herself. "Come on baby," she said in a whisper. "Come to Momma." As Rusty watched the smoke drift off the smouldering cigarette, he felt embarrassed. The woman was a kook.

Chapter Nine

Rusty lay in his Dallas hotel bed and stared at the television. The room was hot and still, not much more than a square closet with an en suite and air-con that blasted only arctic wind or summer heat.

You should go out.

You should find a club in Dallas.

He scanned his phone for a gig listing.

Nothing.

Eva said she'd call and Rusty knew he was waiting for her despite everything. It took another hour, but he got dressed eventually. He was out of beer.

. . .

Rusty walked in no fixed direction until he came to a sports bar. It was nestled in the sub-basement of a hotel and it was crowded for a Sunday night. Middle-aged dads sat at the bar while dozens of younger people in summer shorts and singlet tops took to the adjoining booths. Rusty chose the bar.

He drank and checked his phone.

No sign of Eva.

He messaged Charger, first telling him he was trapped in a dungeon, asking him to notify the authorities. He followed up with another message saying he was fine and back tomorrow.

No reply.

Eventually, Rusty got talking to some kids from across the room as they hovered around the bar. They all had foreign accents. A German girl in an iridescent bootleg Nirvana t-shirt told Rusty there was a backpackers hostel upstairs. Rusty asked if she had a weed connection and she asked around but none of them smoked. When they were gone, one of the dads at the bar said, "I thought the whole point of backpacking was to get high. Sorry, I was eavesdropping."

"I never did it," said Rusty. "Not the world's best traveller."

"I went out when I was in my twenties," said the dad. "It was probably the best time of my life. It's not too late for you, you know." He laughed to himself. "You want another?"

Rusty shrugged.

The dad ordered another round and said, "And I'll tell you another thing, it was good all right, but it didn't make me happy."

Chapter Ten

Rusty's phone chimed in the night, vibrating across the floor of the hotel bathroom inside the pocket of his jeans. Ava called twice before he found it, and when he did, the screen lit the room.

"Did I wake you?" she said.

"What time is it?"

He turned the bathroom light on and squinted at himself in the mirror. He looked terrible, like his own Halloween mask.

Ava said, "A few things came to me after you left but I forgot to call. I fell asleep. I had a dream and I think it was about your guitar."

"Okay."

"I was asleep on the pavement outside a building. It was in Chelsea, Manhattan. That's definitely where I was. I got up and walked along the street until I came to this orange door, no sign or anything, just a plain orange door. I went inside and after a little corridor, I stepped into a house of mirrors, like at a county fair or something, a room that had all these mirrors reflecting into one another. I was frightened, so I tried to get out of there, but I couldn't. And then..." The sharp flicker of Ava's cigarette lighter sounded. "And then the lights above started switching on and off. Light, dark, light, dark. When it went dark, a word hung in the air, some trick of the light, like if you stare at a word on a blank page and then stare at a wall, you sometimes see the word. Anyway, more words came and the words spelled out a sentence. It said the same thing over and over. It said, *You can't see anything at all.* And then. *All you see is me.* Does that mean anything to you?"

"No," said Rusty. "Was that the end?"

"Almost. When the lights flashed on, I was one person, and when they were off, I was someone else. I just knew it somehow. This is where it gets kind of weird—"

"It's already plenty—"

"I had a glass eye in the dream. So I took it out and looked at myself. Through the eye, I was *you*, Rusty. Exactly you, from this afternoon. But in the mirror, I was a woman. I didn't recognize her, but as soon as I woke up, I knew it was your sister. Do you have a sister?"

"Yes," he said.

"Was her name Anna?"

Rusty removed the phone from his ear. He could hear Ava's voice in the tiny speaker. He put the phone back to his ear and said, "I had a sister. She's been dead a couple of years. Her name was Anna."

"That's... it's not normally this specific."

"What does this have to do with the guitar?"

"None of this stuff ever has much to do with the actual thing, not in my experience. It's just stuff. My advice is, you need to get rid of the guitar. It's not a bad omen, exactly, but it's not good either."

"It's never felt right," he said.

Neither of them spoke. Rusty turned off the bathroom light and stood there in the darkness. "Maybe I should just dump it?"

"No, that's not it. You need to send it on."

"Send it where?"

"I don't know. You need a guitar expert, not a psychic."

Chapter Eleven

Rusty's job at the university tech office was part-time and, within reason, he could move his days around. With sick days on top, he figured he had a week before anyone would notice he was interstate. This became a deadline of sorts. He had a week to get rid of the guitar.

In quick succession, he booked a flight to New York and, embracing the full romance of an impromptu trip, he organized a three-night stay at the Chelsea Hotel. There seemed no point resisting this any further. He either believed Ava and her Manhattan dream or he didn't, and with his credit card in hand, phone cradled to his jaw, Rusty found he took Ava at her word.

He trusted Ava because he trusted Anna. Rusty had lived his whole life with his sister. He had held her hand as she died in a hospital bed in the middle of the night. The next day — as if a switch were hit — she was gone. Had disappeared. Rusty now struggled to remember her as a whole person, to see her back before to her last days. It was like his forgotten months this year, which is how he ended up in Dallas. And yet today, Anna was back, almost in the room with him, all because of the orange guitar.

By the time Rusty landed in New York, he had an email from Ava full of notes. She wrote well, and her account of the dream was vivid. She described the streets, the peeling paintwork of the orange door, the house of mirrors beyond. She detailed his sister's appearance in painful and accurate ways. According to Ava, Anna wore a paper nightgown, one that matched her bone white skin. She had a thick black watch strapped to her wrist. It was the final Anna. The hospital version. The skeleton.

In the Chelsea Hotel, Rusty searched the internet and made a plan. There was no House of Mirrors on the whole of Manhattan island, nor anything that resembled the room Ava described, but Ava had a rough idea where she was from a previous visit to New York. The street she saw was somewhere in the Tribeca district.

The previous day, Rusty walked the streets in a grid but couldn't find an orange door in the whole neighbourhood. As dark came on, he resorted to running chunks of Ava's email through Google, but the message she saw floating in the air in her dream was a dead end.

You can't see anything at all.

All you see is me.

Nothing, not a single hit.

None of it was real. The mirrors didn't really exist, nor the door or the room or Ava's glass eye. It was all metaphor and trance.

Frustrated, Rusty scanned a dream dictionary online and found, *When you dream of mirrors, you dream of the multiple inner selves within you. When you see another in the mirror, you dream of the loss of self and your dream is telling you to reclaim what is lost. You need to take action or responsibility or assert yourself. Insert yourself back into the world.*

It made no sense to Rusty.

He took another beer from the hotel minibar and cracked it open. He looked at himself in the mirror. Another drunken idiot lost in the world, except in the Chelsea Hotel of all places. Rusty laughed and looked worse.

The following morning, he woke dry-mouthed and sick. When he was done vomiting into the toilet basin, he looked up at the bathroom mirror and noticed words there in black marker. Last night, in his stupor, he'd written:

I can't see anything at all.

All I see is me.

He had inserted himself into Ava's message, as the dream dictionary suggested. It sounded familiar.

Rusty went and turned his laptop on.

Chapter Twelve

The guitar tech told him to bring the thing down and he'd check it out. The man had a basement apartment in Brooklyn, a long dank space that was once the building owner's private garage. "Sorry about the mess. There's no cleaning it," the guitar tech said. By the look of it, he had taken this to heart elsewhere in his life. He had long greying hair enveloping his beard, and his beard matched the wiry chest hair springing from his unbuttoned shirt. "You want a drink?" he said. "You look like you need one."

It was ten-thirty in the morning.

"Sure."

Rusty sat in a stray bean bag while the man fixed cocktails from an electric camp fridge. Then he took Rusty's guitar case and laid it open on the bench. He took a sip of his Bloody Mary and nodded. "Yep, that's one of 'em," said the man. "Like you said on the phone."

"Really?"

"Lee played these back in the day and they all went with the truck that night. Jesus, I even recognize this one. See this bridge pickup, see how someone's slotted in a single coil here where there's obviously room for two. This is on the list. I'm sure of it. How did you find it?"

"Ebay," said Rusty.

"I keep hearing that they're out there. It's weird to think. How did you figure it out? This paint job is terrible, but it looks like a regular guitar to most people, I'd imagine."

"I went to a clairvoyant."

The man nodded along, as if this were routine. "And she told you what this was?"

"In a way. She had a dream where she saw this message in the air. *I can't see anything at all, all I see is me.*"

"That's *Eric's Trip*, ain't it?"

"Yeah. I googled it."

The man laughed. "And then you called me?'

Rusty nodded, sipped his drink.

"Lee's gonna love this," he said.

Chapter Thirteen

On July 2nd, 1999, New York band Sonic Youth played a show in Berkley, California. They were on a short tour of the US, a stopgap of sorts between 1998's *A Thousand Leaves* and 2000's *NYC Ghosts and Flowers*. That night in Berkley, they played songs from each album, adding a scattering of their back catalogue, something that ran sixteen years deep at that point. All their songs required an arsenal of odd equipment: modified guitars with strings tuned in unison, guitar bodies scratched open and hacked at with screwdrivers and drumsticks. They made their music with broken, hot-rodded gear played through boutique effects pedals, some of which never made it into commercial production. In short, the equipment the band used was unique. It was part of the show and part of how they made such a distinctive sound. Rusty did not know all this by heart, but had heard about it, and read more online in the Chelsea before coming down.

"It all went that night in Berkley," said Lee in his apartment a few hours later. Lee played guitar in the band. The orange guitar sat on the coffee table between them, the headstock propped up on a pile of books about photography. Lee lent back into his lounge. This was his guitar. He didn't look like much of a rock star to Rusty. The apartment was nice but there were no gold records on the walls, very few traces of Sonic Youth, and even less of Lee as a celebrity. What he had, was a good collection of guitars. They decorated the apartment like homeware.

Lee pointed a thumb at the tech, who sat out on the apartment terrace. "While he was asleep in this lousy motel in Orange County, someone stole the truck from out front. It had everything in it. Thirty guitars, all our amps, dozens of pedals, all that stuff. It was all the gear we'd been playing for years. There are songs we still can't play because of what happened."

"Did they ever find any of it?" said Rusty.

"Not really. Bits and pieces. A guitar here and there. Stuff like this. But the main collection is still out there. These kids sent us photos of it once. It was all there. Just our stuff in a room. The police had a few ideas, but nothing ever came of it. We do okay but we don't really have the resources to hire our own people."

"So you started again?"

"That's right. We bought new gear. It worked out. The whole thing probably gave us more than it took."

"That's crazy."

"I'll say," said the tech. He stepped inside to light a cigarette away from the wind.

Lee said, "Everything comes and goes, don't you think?"

The tech got his light. He took a step back to the terrace, blew a cloud of smoke out. "That stuff just went and went." With that, he took himself back out and closed the door.

"He still feels bad about it," said Lee.

"But you don't?"

"I miss some of it. But that doesn't mean the

songs don't exist, even if I can't play them. Nothing ever really disappears. Some little flourish of things hangs around. That's what I think."

Lee's phone buzzed on the coffee table. He checked the screen, but didn't answer it. When it stopped, he sat there a moment and looked at the orange finish. "You've got to introduce me to this woman," he said. "The psychic. She sounds great."

"She's pretty interesting. Not what you'd think. She's a fiend for eBay, though. Worse than me. Maybe she could keep an eye out for your stuff?"

"I've tried buying gear on eBay, but you know what? I still love guitar stores. You go to a guitar store, pick something up... it's better. It has a story. Online is great for some things but, if you think about it, the story is always the same."

"Really?"

"Okay, okay," he said. "It's *usually* the same."

Lee walked over to a bookshelf covered in small things. He picked up his wallet. "I need to go to an ATM."

Together the three of them left the apartment. Later that day, as the tech danced slowly by himself on the dance floor of a musty bar, Lee remembered the money and the reason they'd stepped out in the first place. He took out a small pile of bills and bought the guitar back from Rusty, then ordered another round.

Chapter Fourteen

It was late but Charger was waiting for him on the couch when Rusty got back to Nevada. Charger had a new plan for his future. He was excited about it. He said, "I'm going to drink milk with every meal and do these new power squats I saw on TV. I've been doing it since you left and it's going great. I'm going to be epic. You should try it."

"Maybe," said Rusty. "Is Katrina around?"

"Nah. You should call her sister, though. She keeps bringing it up."

Rusty sat down. They watched the TV.

"I see you offloaded the guitar," said Charger.

"I did," and Rusty told him the rest.

Charger wasn't impressed. "I don't understand what that was all about," he said, and it took a few minutes to settle in for him. When it had, he rubbed his face and took a cushion and threw it on the floor by the couch. He went to it and began a set of sit-ups.

Rusty rolled off the couch and held Charger's feet.

"What are you going to do now?" Charger said.

"Nothing. That's it."

Chapter Fifteen

On his first day back at work, Rusty called Ava Wells. She didn't pick up at first, but he called again.

"What?"

"Ava, it's Rusty."

"Uh-huh."

"I got rid of the guitar like you said."

"Good. How do you feel?"

"I don't know. Better, I guess."

"The story was better than the thing itself, wasn't it?"

"Yeah."

"Did you talk to your sister?"

"No. I told you, she's dead. She died two years ago. Cancer."

"Oh that's right. Well, I guess you have to get rid of that too," Ava said.

Rusty wheeled back from his desk. He put his head down against his knees.

Ava said, "Did you call me for advice or just for a chat? Because, look, you can *know* everything, Rusty, and still have nothing, just like you can *have* everything, all the prizes of online shopping and whatever, and still end up with jack shit. There's no difference. Happiness is about what you can let go of, that's it. That's why dumb people are happy."

"Are you sure?"

"It's the only thing I'm sure of."

Rusty said goodbye and put the phone down.

As the coffee machine buzzed, he thought more about Ava's advice. Some of it worked and some of it didn't. Forgetting things did not seem to make him happy, and that's how all this got started. Forgetting his sister didn't work. It seemed to him now that there must be a great difference between forgetting and letting go.

A voice snapped Rusty out of his daze. "Hello?"

Elsa stood over at the counter. "I had to

come in and see someone in student admin," she said.

He went over, looked her up and down.
"What?"

"Nothing," said Rusty, but she'd finally changed out of her pyjamas.

END

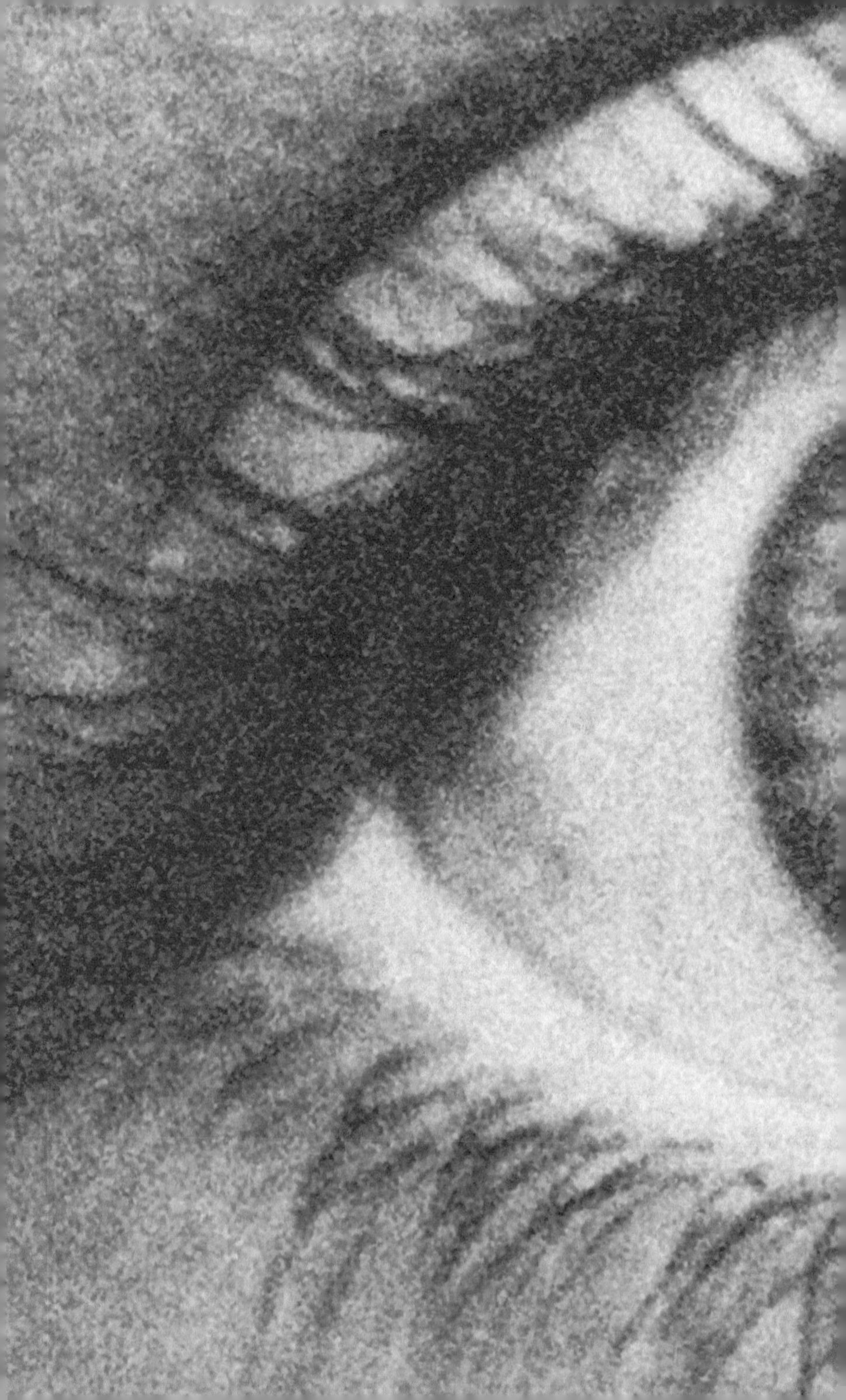

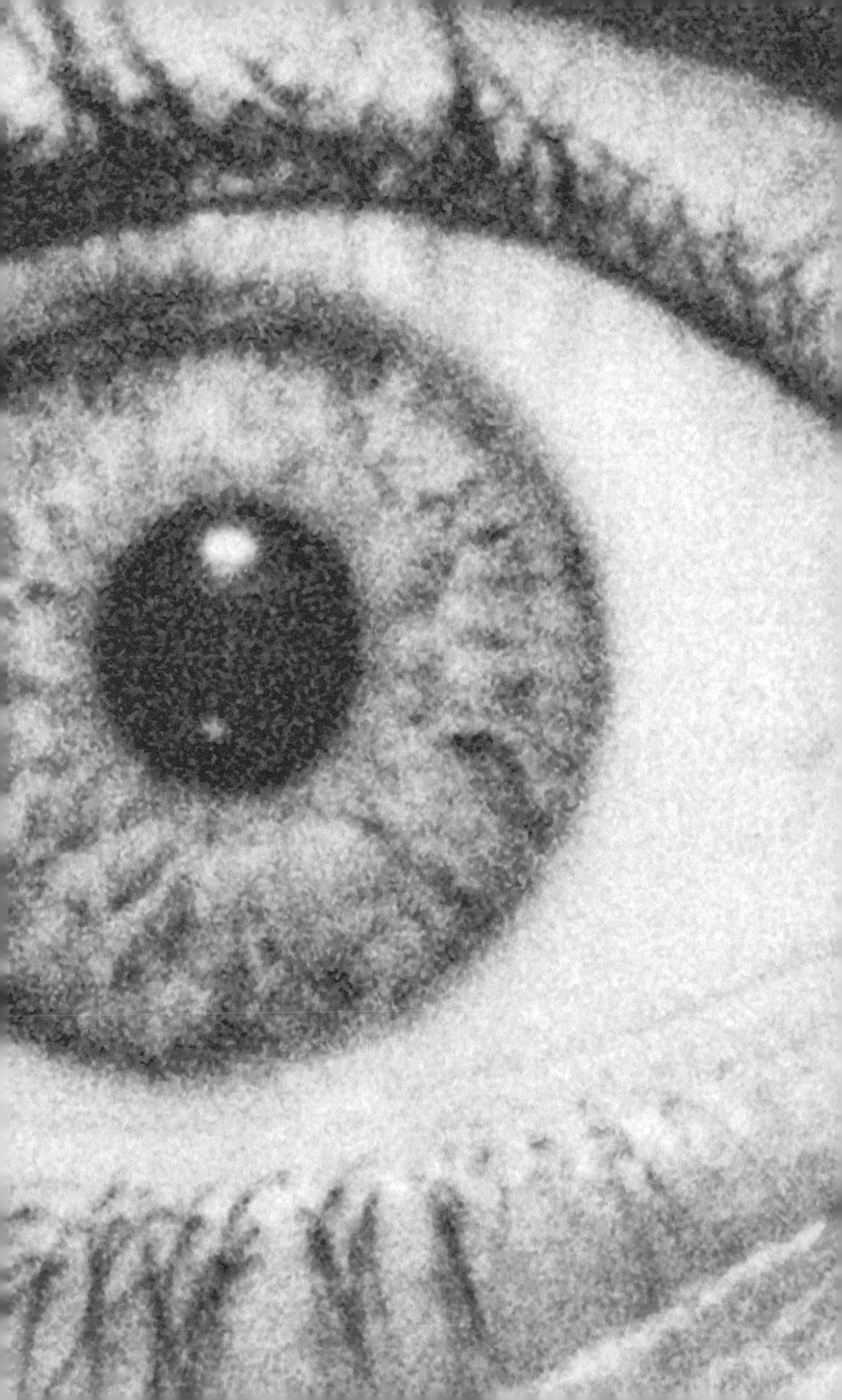

THE DRIFTER

In reality, time doesn't pass. We pass.

— Ken Bruen

Chapter One

The drifter pulled off the road onto the gravel and waited. Two hours out of the city and everything had fallen away. There was only the highway now, the dirt planes either side. He stepped out the sedan and drank the last of his coffee. It was quiet. It was dark.

He walked to the desert.

His phone chimed.

"Yeah?"

The old man on the line said, "Is that how you answer the phone? With yeah? What, ya raised by wolves or something?"

"What do you want?"

"Just checking in, ya know. That money went through."

"I got the message."

"You get the number? Eight. Nine. Four. Seven. Hash."

"I said I got it." The drifter looked around, unbuttoned his fly. "Are we done here?"

Chapter Two

The drifter ended up back in L.A. after his conscience got the better of him. He knew he'd done harm in his life, but the weight of specific things made no sense to him. The stealing, the cheating, some of the fighting, none of that brushed up against him. That's just what happened. What he couldn't quite shake was what happened with Cale and his wife.

They'd all lived together in the same cottage out in East L.A. Cale still lived there, still owned the place. When the drifter called, he didn't even sound that surprised. "I always wondered when you'd turn up," he said.

The drifter showed up at the house and Cale showed him around like he'd never been there before. Cale had renovated and painted, but it was still the same. There was a shed in the yard now. *Her shed.* Something to do with her work. Cale opened the shed door, and they looked in on her desk and everything about her came back to the drifter. It smelled like her. A lot of her things remained: books, a yellow pad, an old calendar. Cale said he didn't have much need for a writing desk, but sometimes he liked to go out there and listen to the radio.

Back in the house, Cale took two beers from the refrigerator and they drank them in front of the game. Cale said, "You ever end up getting married?"

"Nearly. One time," said the drifter.

"It's not the easiest thing in the world, is it? Still feels strange without her. I get bored. Never used to get bored. You get bored?"

"Sometimes."

Cale seemed comfortable enough just sitting there. He let the drifter smoke inside and didn't seem to mind the fresh ash in his dead wife's ashtray. The drifter looked at Cale watching the game and said, "I'm real sorry I never came back for the funeral."

"Just how things are sometimes," Cale said and smiled a little. "She wasn't here to miss you, buddy."

"It worries me," said the drifter.

"What? Dying?"

"No. Not coming back. I think you and her were... you know, family."

Cale waited, then he said, "Well kid, you don't get to pick who you do your bit with, do you?"

Chapter Three

That night the drifter slept on Cale's couch in his underwear. It was September, and a shower came through. He went to the kitchen and took a glass of water. Out past the yard, on the neighbour's house, a bright light shone like a spotlight and in it the drifter could see the rain coming down. It was heavy, but it seemed to hang in the air. The drifter could feel himself staring at it. Cale's wife told him once that she loved him, right here in this house. She said it quickly, quietly, under her breath, like she didn't want either of them to hear it. It happened in the bedroom right beside the kitchen, just through the wall, right where

Cale slept at this very moment. It might have been the same bed. Maybe he never bought a new one?

Chapter Four

The drifter only stayed the night, but he saw Cale at a bar a couple of days later and that's when Cale told him he needed money. He had gambling debts. He'd taken it up again. It was all going wrong. Cale would have to re-mortgage the house and was in a bad way about it.

"How much do you need?" said the drifter.

Cale shrugged.

"Well, work it out then."

Cale took a notebook from his jacket and flicked through it. He had a pencil and started transferring numbers across. When he was done, he said, "If the Seahawks win by fifteen tonight, it'll be... let me see."

The drifter leaned over and checked the page. "Sixty grand? Christ, Cale."

"Sixty if the Hawks win. Sixty-two if my luck holds."

"Shit."

"That's about the long and the short of it."

Cale waved at the barmen, pointed for another. When he looked at the drifter, he saw it immediately. "No, no. What? You think you're gonna give me the money? This isn't your problem, kid. Snap out of it."

"I figure, I owe you. I could get it."

"What do you owe me for?" Cale said.

"You fucking know."

"But I love to hear you say it. Come on, just one more time before you disappear on me again. Just one more time." This was a thing he used to do. "Come on. Tell me."

"Okay. You ready?"

"Yep. Lay it on me."

"Cale, thank you for saving my ass in prison."

Cale laughed so hard people started looking. "Really? Is that what I did? It was so long ago I almost forgot."

"Thank god one of us could fight back then," said the drifter.

"Yeah, it sure came in handy in there, but I'm not as good as I used to be."

That was probably true. Cale was old now and life had drawn a lot of the violence out of him, by the look of it. Life can do that. But Cale had a lot of violence in him to begin with. Vast reserves of it. The drifter once saw him beat a man to death in the prison yard. He took the guy from behind, pulled him into a corner and used a loose piece of brickwork. It took a minute, start to finish. When it was done, Cale dropped the body and walked to the other wall where the inmates crowded around. The drifter could still see it in his mind's eye. He could see Cale squatting on the ground, washing the blood off his hands with a canteen.

Chapter Five

Later that night, the drifter took a walk through the old neighbourhood. It'd been a long time and things had changed, but overall, it was still about the same. One shitty convenience store pasted over another. Two apartment blocks where one had been. New billboards for the same old shit. All the same clutter and rubbish threaded through the same alleyways and street corners. Fucking L.A. The whole city reminded him of the back of a restaurant.

The drifter came up on a dusty-looking gas station. The attendant had the game on. He sat on a stool, slumped against the shelves of cigarettes, his shirt front stretched across his gut.

"Who's in front?" asked the drifter.

"Not the Hawks."

The drifter bought a beer and broke a bill.

He went out to a pay phone and made the call.

A woman answered.

The drifter said, "I'm looking for Ray."

Big Ray was a local kid he used to know, weighed about one twenty pounds, used to live with his mother, Little Ray. Big Ray came on the line with a weary, "Yeah, what do you want?"

"It's Eric Hendricks."

"Oh goody. What do *you* want, mother-fucker? It's been a minute."

The drifter told him and it turned out that Big Ray knew all about Cale's money problems. It was Big Ray who was taking Cale's bets these days. He'd moved up in the world. Big Ray said the figures in Cale's notebook were about right, but to his credit, Big Ray wasn't too fussy about who paid up. "I don't give a fuck. You wanna spring up out of nowhere for that old man, it's none of my business."

"Can you hook me up?" said the drifter.

"You wanna *work* this off?" said Ray. "That's interesting."

"You want the money, Ray?"

"Yeah, I do, I do."

"Then put me on."

"For the whole amount?"

"That's right."

"Okay. You got a pen? I know a guy," he said. "There's something coming in."

"Yeah, I got a pen," said the drifter.

Chapter Six

The drifter waited by the baseball diamond in Garvey Park and smoked a cigarette. When the guy arrived, he seemed to appear out of nowhere on the far side of the field. Just another old man in the bleachers, looking like he'd always been there. As the drifter walked round, he watched the man through the netting. He was thin, white, wearing a fleecy camping jacket and wrap-around sunglasses. He had a thermos by his side. Sixty-plus, but looked strong for his age, like he would have been real trouble not long ago and just regular trouble now.

The drifter said, "Are you Big Ray's guy?"

"I'm no one's guy, shithead. Sit down. Ya don't look so good?"

The drifter did it.

"Roll up them sleeves," said the man. He had a look. "Okay. Now, show me ya hands. Turn 'em over." The old man looked at them, handling him like he was livestock. "Ya good with cars from what I hear. That's what Ray told me."

The drifter nodded.

"Well, this is what I need. It's pretty simple. These people I know..." The old man stopped, looked around. "These people, they have three drops. All of 'em out of town. All on the same day. It's in a straight line. All cash, no drugs, all in parked cars. You can deal with the cars, right?"

"Yeah."

"They're usually utilities. Shitty ones."

"Okay."

"So ya get yourself out to the first one. Don't take ya own ride, take the bus. Boost the car and then drive it to the next drop and stash it where we tell ya to stash it. There's three like that, so ya do it three times. Last drop is a bus terminal. Ya get on a bus and fuck off and that's that."

"How's my end going to work?" said the drifter.

"Ya split is seventy-five, take it or leave it. Ya need some of it now?"

"No, I'm good. But sixty goes to Ray when I'm done with the second car."

"Okay, I can probably handle that," said the old man.

"Is this Ray's job?"

"What? Big Ray doesn't know his asshole from a hole in the ground." The old man stared out at the field. "I think this'll work. I'll give ya a number to dial in case of trouble." He stood up, looking down at the drifter square on. "Do I need to say it?"

"Probably not," said the drifter.

"Do exactly what I just said."

"Yeah, I've been around."

"I hope so. It's happening the day after tomorrow." The old man stood there and waited some more. "Ya gonna have to leave first," he said.

Chapter Seven

When the drifter woke, it was dark out. He took a beer from the minibar and showered. He dressed up a little and walked to a bar. In a booth by the window, he called the only local girl in his phone. Alice. She answered, but she didn't want to see him. Alice had a kid now.

He ordered another drink and thought about Cale and the old man in the park. Something about the old man scanned wrong. Most of it was okay — the way he spoke, the way he just sat there on the bleachers — but there was something else. It'd been a while since he'd been in this world, but his gut told him this job was something worse than just stealing money and cars.

There was some other loose end the drifter couldn't quite see. He sipped his drink as he dialled Cale's number and got the answering machine. It was her voice telling him they weren't home.

The dead wife.

"What the fuck, Cale? Why do you still have that on there?" he said.

They had gotten together slowly. It wasn't some lonely housewife thing. She wasn't looking for trouble, and they were both scared of Cale back then. But it was one of those things that happened anyway. Living together didn't help. Familiarity sped it up. And it felt fated, like it always going to happen. There the very first time they met.

When the drifter got out of prison, Cale was working and couldn't pick him up from the bus terminal, so he sent her instead. The drifter knew her to look at — Cale had shown him pictures in the joint — but she was different in the flesh. She drove a brown station wagon with the windows down, her hair blowing around, a bare arm catching the sun. At one point, she took two cigarettes from a pack on the dashboard and lit them with the dashboard lighter. "Hey kid," she said. "Here," and she took one from her mouth and handed it to him.

"Thanks."

She tugged at her shirt collar. A thin pale neck. A reddish tint in her hair at the back. She didn't have make-up on. He watched her put both hands on the steering wheel and glance into the rear-view mirror. Then she looked at him and laughed. "Been a while huh? Didn't anyone visit you up there?"

"Nah."

The drifter stayed with them for four months until Cale got him a job in a warehouse. Cale kept an eye on him. For a long time, a year or so, the drifter didn't even think about jumping out of line. He didn't need to because she was around. She was worth staying straight for.

Then things picked up. After the drifter got his own place, Cale switched to night shift. She'd come round while Cale was working and he'd fix her dinner. They'd eat and talk a little and then they'd fuck. Afterward, she'd put her running sweats back on and go home. Six months it went on, and it was the happiest six months of his entire life. Looking back, he could see now that he was so delirious and insane with her that it blinded him. Their affair was anything but a miracle. They were making and re-making a terrible mistake every time. Both of them dozing naked in his humid little apartment, half-smoked cigarettes smouldering away, all while the man who helped them both through the worst possible shit drove a forklift around a back lot not ten minutes across town.

Chapter Eight

On the day of the job, the drifter did exactly as the old man said. He checked out of the motel on dusk and caught a bus to Lancaster and followed the directions to the first car. It was a battered old tray-back truck. It sat in the centre of a car park by a hospital. The drifter didn't like the look of it at first. In his text messages, the old man hadn't been specific about the timing — he just wanted it all done in succession — so the drifter waited a while. He took the elevator up to a canteen in the hospital and bought a sandwich. He lit a cigarette and went to the balcony and watched the car for an hour. He scanned nearby buildings and looked at the windows and judged things. It would take about two minutes and there were traffic lights not far up the road. The timing was hard to predict.

The drifter took the lift back down and walked out to the truck. He used a slim jim, popped the door, got in and checked the ignition, then laughed. He rammed a flathead screwdriver into the keyhole and started the engine. No finesse required.

It was about four hours to Bullhead City and the next pickup. He took it easy. Whoever was supposed to collect the drop must have been expecting a drive because the tank was full. It started to rain about an hour out of town, and the drifter took it as a good omen. Rain kept people focused on what they were doing. It kept their eyes off other people. It was the best weather to pull stuff like this.

At a roadside toilet, he called Cale and waited through his dead wife's answering message again. At the tone he said, "Cale, it's me. Call me back."

The first drop went off as planned. The place was right where they said it would be. The drifter drove into a single space garage out by the airport and rolled down the door. Clean. He didn't see another person until he got to the airport shuttle where there was a bus already waiting. When the bus was out on the road and the drifter was surer of the other passengers, all six of them, he walked up the aisle to the little washroom. He took his time inside, washed his face and hands. In the little mirror, he checked himself. He was fine. His eyes had a trace of fear in them, but you had to know him to see it. The tell wasn't half as bad as it could have been.

In the joint, Cale looked after him for no real reason. He didn't fuck him. He didn't ask him to make the beds. He didn't use him to cop or to steal or to do anything like that. Cale was right when he joked about their time together: the drifter was too white and too pretty for prison, and it could have gone real bad if Cale hadn't stepped in. Shit, he was getting turned out by a cellmate when he first met Cale. Had already sold himself to the guy for a couple of favours without even knowing it. "Tomorrow they're going to ask you to pay up," Cale said. "Then when you can't, they'll offer you an out and if you don't take it, they'll come at you, and short of killing one of them, you'll have to give them what they were after all along." The drifter was only in for a three-year stretch for a car. He couldn't kill someone. So Cale paid them off, and he had enough favours with the brotherhood to back it up. Even when Cale got out, they let him alone. That's just how Cale was back then.

The drifter went back to his bus seat and looked out the windows. Off in the distance, he could see Vegas in the downpour.

Chapter Nine

The second drop was a sedan. It was at another hospital and that made him wonder. He felt like he couldn't afford to be cautious the second time, so he walked past the car once then opened it. He used a pick on the ignition. It started easy enough. Hip hop blasted out of the stereo the moment the engine turned over. The drifter turned it off. Whoever these people were, it wasn't a tight ship.

Out on the highway, the old man sent a message. It was an address in Provo, an apartment garage, same deal. The drifter messaged back that he was in the car and that meant Cale's debts with Big Ray were squared away. He felt good about that. He drove faster. He even stopped at a gas station and bought a coffee and a fresh pack. Then he turned the stereo back on. It was a good couple of hours before the rain stopped and before the phone booth caught his eye. It was the *same* phone booth. And having seen it, he couldn't shake it. He thought it would be gone by now, ripped down and replaced with something else.

He pulled the car round and drove back. The booth was an old glass panelled number on the edge of a disused gas station. Inside a bulb hummed and flickered overhead. The phone didn't work, someone had cut the cord long ago, but the rest of thing was there, like some fucked-up monument. The drifter stood there in the dry and looked at the phone and the surrounding walls. He checked the slot for change. He wiped the glass and tried to remember what the gas station used to look like. He tried to remember everything except the call he made here. But then he couldn't just stand there and not think about it. It was impossible. This was the place. This was the last time he ever heard her say something.

Chapter Ten

In June ninety-nine, she started talking about leaving Cale. They'd been sneaking around for almost a year and the anniversary of it meant something to her. It was time for a change, she said. Cale couldn't see it coming. The way he was, he didn't understand people too well, not deep down. Cale expected people to be the same all the time, *not to* change. If someone did the wrong thing by him in the pen, he was always surprised at first. Of course, he suspected everyone he needed to be wary of but people closer in, they often caught him off guard. It was one of the few ways the drifter could help him. The drifter just knew when someone was lying, he could sense trouble a mile off. So Cale probably saw no difference in his wife the whole time they were together. As long as she was around when he expected her to be, and as long as she spoke the same way and looked the same, Cale just assumed everything was okay.

It came to a head when the anniversary was a week away. She just wouldn't let it go. That's when it got real bad. She talked and talked more and more about leaving Cale. She still loved Cale, she said. They both did. But to her, there was no choice. They'd leave together, and he'd be angry, and then, eventually, Cale would forget about her and find someone else.

"I want to grow old with you," she said. "I can't stand not being with you. It feels like not being with you is worse than anything else."

She was right. That's how it felt. "But I can't do it," he said.

She shook her head. "You don't have to. We'll just go. Neither of us can tell him."

"I can't do that either. I can't just take off with his wife."

"I'm not a piece of furniture. To him, maybe."

"You know that's not true."

"I know," she said quietly and that was the worst moment.

As she left that night, she decided they would sleep on it one more time. If she felt the same in the morning, they'd start packing.

And that was it almost. He stayed up all that night, pushing the idea around. No matter how he looked at it, certain things couldn't budge. He knew he could barely live without her, that it made him sick to think of losing her, but he also realised the choice was between doing that to Cale or doing it to himself. That was what it came down to. Once he got to that place, it was clear. If they ran away together, he'd think about Cale every day. He'd never be able to look at her and not remember everything else. There'd be no peace in it.

So he threw it all away. Pretty easy in the doing. He ditched work and got in touch with his pot dealer and the dealer put him in touch with Big Ray and, like always, like the times before prison, Big Ray knew someone who had something and it would be enough to stake him to leave town. Big Ray said these guys over on the southside needed a truck for something they had in the pipe. All he had to do was pick one up and drive it over and they'd do the rest. It took a while, but he found a Ryder truck parked out front of a motel in Orange County, drove it over to University Park and told Ray he wasn't going any further downtown. A guy came and met him in a backstreet and paid the money. The only funny part of it: the guy at the meet had a banged-up face, bandages, early forties maybe, not the sort of guy you normally sell a stolen truck to. Not an inconspicuous sort of guy. Anyway, after it was done, the drifter took a cab back to his car and headed out of the city, out onto the highway he was driving now. He stopped at this phone booth right here and called her. All he said, over and over again, was how sorry he was. She was hysterical. It wasn't like her at all. She was usually so in control of everything, but not then. At some point all he could do was stop talking and hang up.

Chapter Eleven

The drifter buttoned up his fly and stood there, out on the planes behind the phone booth and the ruins of the gas station. In the distance, the sun edged up from behind the mountains and it started to make colour in the desert.

He looked at his phone. It had been five minutes since the old man's call, time to decide. Dump the car and run, or dump the car and finish it.

"Fuck it."

He walked back to the road. It wasn't like the world would fall apart over one more stolen car.

Chapter Twelve

The next drop went mostly like the old man said it would. He drove the car into Provo and found the street and the apartment building. As he came up on it, a man stepped out of the garage and waved him in. The man was big and soft-looking, in sweatpants, his gut hanging out the front. The drifter turned off the engine, got out and walked past the man, gave him a nod, and crossed the street.

He jumped a cab from the main road down to the next address where he took a moment to stand out on the street and look it over. The car was on the top level of a carpark by a church. The carpark was a big three-level place that needed a fresh coat of paint and some new signage. The neighbouring church didn't look so hot either: half of it had fallen in on itself and a team of men moved around the remains on scaffolding. It was early morning. They must have just got started. The builders shouted to each other as they dropped masonry down into a skip by the curb. The drifter looked from the church to the carpark and checked the angles. They seemed okay. He didn't like the noise, but at least they couldn't see him boost the car.

He stubbed his cigarette out and thought about calling Cale again, then thought better of it. He crossed the street and went in, walked up the concrete ramps. The place was virtually empty, especially higher up. As the roof opened, the drifter ducked off to the side and climbed a railing to check for problems up top. The lot was empty except for a single green hatchback parked in the centre. The drifter dropped back down and thought on it: *run or walk?* It was an older car. It'd open fast. He unzipped his knapsack and went through a roll of master keys. He had the one.

He walked.

It took about a minute to get to the car.

It was empty.

He circled it and checked underneath.

It was clean.

The drifter put his hand in his pocket and pulled out the key. The lock took. He got in and fired up the engine, drove slowly down the park's long interior spiral. The car sounded like it could use a service, but it handled okay. At street level, a boom gate lay across the exit. The drifter punched in the code he was given in the desert by the old man.

Eight.

Nine.

Four.

Seven.

Hash.

He looked down and checked the gearbox and edged the car forward.

The boom stayed in place.

He took the car out of gear and re-checked his phone. The code was right. He punched it in again.

Eight.

Nine.

Four.

Light flickered in front of the car.

A cracking sound.

At first, he thought it was the builders, but then he saw the man and the gun and the second shot came through. The windscreen splintered. There was blood on it. The drifter accelerated and slammed the car into the boom gate, then reversed hard, something tumbling under the car as he went. He couldn't see the shooter but whoever it was fired again, and part of the windscreen fell away. The drifter put the car in gear and drove out the entryway, swerving onto the street and around a double-parked van by the church. As he sped up, he checked the rear-view: a man out on the street.

More shots echoed.

They sounded like fireworks.

Chapter Thirteen

Back in the desert, back towards L.A., the drifter felt blood spread across his side. He came to his senses enough to realise how messed up the windscreen was. He turned off into a side road and looked for a place to pull over. Suddenly thirsty, he took another adjacent road down to what looked like a lake where he slammed the car into a gravel embankment on the water's edge.

He kicked the door open. As soon as he stood up, he realised things were worse than he thought. The hole in his side didn't look so bad, there wasn't blood gushing out everywhere, but it still hurt plenty. He hobbled down to the water and drank.

That's when he started to feel faint. He sat up, but found he couldn't stay steady. He put his head down for a moment and slumped over. With his face in the dirt, he was sure he could hear an engine working. Maybe he'd left the car running? The morning sun seemed hot. He groaned and there was sweat or tears or blood in his eyes.

Chapter Fourteen

The phone woke him and stopped. He couldn't really feel much. The phone buzzed again.

He answered it.

It was the old man. "Where are ya?"

"Fuck you," said the drifter and coughed. "Listen, fuck off, or I'll kill Big Ray and his mom and then I'll come and kill you as well."

"I know who ya are, son. Ya not gonna to do shit. Ya sound half-dead already. Tell me where ya are and we'll come and clean up the mess."

"Yeah, I don't think so."

He put the phone down.

Chapter Fifteen

Later, he looked out at his hand and saw the phone again. The call was still live. He lifted it to his ear.

Nothing.

He called Cale. It rang out.

The answering machine picked up.

The drifter listened to her voice on the machine.

He called her again.

And again.

And maybe Cale picked up at some point or maybe he called someone else — he must have — but eventually she spoke back to him. She sounded young and different, but it was definitely her, the old her. She told him to stop and to listen. She said, "Where are you, sir?" She asked him if he was hurt.

"I've been shot."

She kept telling him to do things. There were all these questions, and he had no idea why she was so interested in his predicament when there was so much else to talk about.

He heard the engine sound again and lifted his head a little. Out of the corner of his eye, he could see the water moving. It looked nice, like a hotel pool.

"Hello?" said Cale's wife on the phone.

"I'm sorry," he said. "I've just never been able to settle since you. I never should have come back, but it's all I've ever wanted. I've just been circling, circling... all this time. Just always moving around thinking I was going forward, but I wasn't. I was just moving around you. Over and over and... over, I don't.... It seems so stupid now."

"Stay with me," she said.

"I can't believe I made the wrong decision."

"Are you there? You have to stay on the line."

"I'm here."

"Good. Keep talking to me."

"I have so much to tell you."

"Good," she said. And then she told him to put his hands over the wound again.

He propped his head up. The motor sound was loud now. He closed his eyes, and when he reopened them, a man stood over him. Hands grabbed at him. The drifter fought them off, frightened. The men took the phone until he cried out for so long they gave it back to him.

She was still on the line. "I'm here, I'm here. It's okay, son. Stay calm."

"Thank god," he said. "I just…"

"Talk to me. Tell me."

"You were the only thing I couldn't steal."

END

Please Review This Book

If you enjoyed this book, please consider reviewing it on Amazon and Goodreads. Reviews help *a lot*. Thanks for reading.

Also by IAIN RYAN

THE STUDENT

Signed copies available at iainryan.com

Gatton, Queensland. 1994. Nate is a student, dealing weed on the side. A girl name Maya Kibby is dead. No one knows who killed her. Nate needs to refresh his supply, but his friend and dealer is missing. Nate is high. He's alone. Being hunted for a suitcase he's found and haunted by its contents. And as things turn from bad to worse, Nate uncovers far more than he bargained for.

The Student is high-paced, hardboiled regional noir:
fresh, gritty, unnerving, with a stark and lonely
beauty.

'The Student takes the campus novel and mines within
it a dark seam of violence, deception and suspense in
prose that burns with a fierce propulsion'

-DAVID WHISH-WILSON

"A gruelling, compelling read that took me on a
journey through rural Australia's dark, drug-fucked
underbelly. *Breaking Bad* meets Andrew McGahan's
Praise meets *Wake in Fright*"

- GARY KEMBLE

THE SPIRAL

Signed copies available at iainryan.com

Erma Bridges' life is far from perfect, but entirely
ordinary. After years of dedication to academic
research, her career is falling apart, all because of a
mysterious workplace complaint. So, when she is shot
twice by Jenny – a vindictive colleague who has
seemingly disappeared – her quiet existence is
shattered in an instant.

With her would-be murderer dead, no one can give

Erma the answers she needs to move on from her trauma. Why her? Why now?

Panicked, overworked and on the verge of a nervous breakdown, Erma begins her quest for the truth – and a dangerous, thrilling journey into the heart of darkness. As a web of brutality unfurls around her, Erma uncovers a dark series of crimes on campus and discovers a side of herself unimaginable within the polite world of academia.

"Ambitious and well-executed."

— THE GUARDIAN

"After more than 50 years of reading, about one book a decade really surprises me, and The Spiral looks like being it for the 20s for me."

— NICK EARLS

"Gripping, inventive and utterly unpredictable."

– ALEX PAVESI

Contact The Author

To contact Iain visit IainRyan.com.

Iain sends out monthly book recommendations to his newsletter.

Subscribe at:
https://iainryan.substack.com/subscribe

 twitter.com/iainkryan

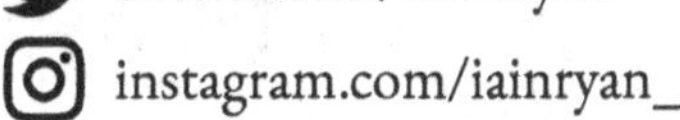 instagram.com/iainryan_

About Iain Ryan

www.iainryan.com

Iain Ryan grew up in the outer suburbs of Brisbane, Australia. He predominantly writes in the hardboiled/noir genre and his work has been published by *Akashic Books Online*, *Crime Factory*, *Kill Your Darlings* and *Seizure*.

Four Days, his first novel, saw release November 2015 via Broken River Books. The following year the book was shortlisted for the Australian Crime Writing Association's Ned Kelly Award (Best Debut Fiction). It didn't win.

A follow up novel titled *The Student* was published in 2017 by Echo Publishing. The following year, the book was shortlisted for The Australian Crime Writing Association's Ned Kelly Award (Best Novel). It didn't win either.

In 2020, Echo Publishing and Bonnier Zaffre (UK) published Ryan's third novel, *The Spiral*.